The Devil Of The Mercato Vecchio

Legends Of Florence

ced Of Florence

Copyright © 2012 Author Name

All rights reserved.

ISBN: 1539118592
ISBN-13: 9781539118596

The Devil Of The Mercato Vecchio

"The Devil sat down in London town
Before earth's morning ray,
With a favourite imp he began to chat,
On religion, and scandal, and this and that,
Until the dawn of day.

THE DEVIL OF THE MERCATO VECCHIO

"Have I not the magic wand, by means of which, having first invoked the spirit Odeken, one can enter the elfin castle? Is not this a fine trot on the devil's crupper? Here it is- one of the palaces erected by rivals of the Romans. Let us enter, for I hold a hand of glory to which all doors open. Let us enter, hic et nunc, the palace fair... Here it was once on a Sabato of the Carnival that there entered four graceful youths of noble air."- Arlecchino alle Nozze di Cana.

I very naturally made inquiry as to whether there was not a legend of the celebrated bronze devil made by Giovanni di Bologna, which remained until lately in the Mercato Vecchio, and I obtained the following, which is, from intrinsic evidence, extremely curious and ancient.

IL DIAVOLO ALLA CAVOLAIA

"On the corner of the Palace Cavolaia there were anciently four devils of iron. These were once four gentlemen who, being wonderfully intimate, had made a strange compact, swearing fidelity and love among themselves to death, agreeing also that if they married, their wives and children and property should be all in common.

"When such vows and oaths are uttered, the saints may pass them by, but the devils hear them; they hear them in hell, and they laugh and cry,

'These are men who will some day be like us, and here for ever!' Such sin as that is like a root which, once planted, may be let alone- the longer it is in the ground, the more it grows. Terra non avvilisceoro- earth does not spoil gold, but even virtue, like friendship, may grow into a great vice

The Devil Of The Mercato Vecchio

when it grows too much.

"As it happened in this case. Well, the four friends were invited to a great festa in that fatal palace of the Cavolaia, and they all went.

And they danced and diverted themselves with great and beautiful ladies in splendour and luxury. As the four were all singularly handsome and greatly admired, the ladies came con grandi tueletti- in their best array, sfarzose per essere corteggiate-

making themselves magnificent to be courted by these gentlemen, and so they looked at one another with jealous eyes, and indeed many a girl there would have gladly been wife to them all, or wished that the four were one, while the married dames wished that they could fare i sposamenti- be loved by one or all.

People were wicked in those days!

"But what was their surprise- and a fearful surprise it was- when, after all their gaiety, they heard at three o'clock in the morning the sound of a bell which they had never heard before, and then divine music and singing, and there entered a lady of such superhuman beauty as held them enchanted and speechless. Now it was known that, by the strict rules of that palace, the festa must soon close, and there was only time for one more dance, and it was sworn among these friends that every lady who danced with one of them, must dance with all in succession. Truly they now repented of their oath, for she was so beautiful.

"But the lady advancing, pointed out one of the four, and said,
'I willdance with him alone.'

"The young signore would have refused, but he felt himself obliged, despite himself, to obey her, and when they had danced, she suddenly disappeared, leaving all amazed.

"And when they had recovered from the spell which had been upon them, they said that as she had come in with the dawn and vanished with the day, it must have been the Beautiful Alba, the enchanting queen of the fairies.

"The festa lasted for three days, and every night at the same hour the beautiful Alba reappeared, enchanting all so wonderfully, that even the ladies forgot their jealousy, and were as much fascinated by her as were the men.

"Now of the four friends, three sternly reproached the other for breaking his oath, they being themselves madly in love; but he replied, and truly, that he had been compelled by some power which he could not resist to obey her. But that, as a man of honour, so far as he could, he would comply with the common oath which bound them.

"Then they declared that he should ask her if she loved him, and if she assented, that he should inform her of their oath, and that she must share her love with all or none- altrimenti non avrebbe mai potuta sposarla.

"Which he did in good faith, and she answered, 'Hadst thou loved me sincerely and fully, thou wouldst have broken that vile oath; and yet it is creditable to thee

The Devil Of The Mercato Vecchio

that, as a man of honour, thou wilt not break thy word. Therefore thou shalt be mine, but not till after a long and bitter punishment. Now I ask thy friends and thee, if to be mine they are willing to take the form of demons and bear it openly before all men.'

"And when he proposed it to his friends, he found them so madly in love with the lady that they, thinking she meant some disguise, declared that to be hers they would willingly wear any form, however terrible.

"And the fair Alba, having heard them, said, 'Yes, ye shall indeed be mine; more than that I do not promise. Now meet me to-morrow at the Canto dei Diavoli- at the Devil's Corner!'

"And they gazed at her astonished, never having heard of such a place. But she replied, 'Go into the street and your feet shall guide you, and truly it will be a great surprise.'

"And they laughed among themselves, saying, 'The surprise will be that she will consent to become a wife to us all.'

"But when they came to the corner, in the night, what was their amazement to see on it four figures of devils indeed, and Alba, who said, 'Now ye are indeed mine, but as for my being yours, that is another matter.'

"Then touching each one, she also touched a devil, and said, 'This is thy form; enter into it. Three of ye shall ever remain as such. As for this fourth youth, he shall be with ye for a year, and then, set free, shall

The Devil Of The Mercato Vecchio

live with me in human form. And from midnight till three in the morning ye also may be as ye were, and go to the Palazzo Cavolaia, and dance and be merry with the rest, but through the day become devils again.'

"And so it came to pass. After a year the image of the chosen lover disappeared; and then one of the three was stolen, and then another, till only one remained."

Legends Of Florence

* * * * *

There is some confusion in the conclusion of this story, which I have sought to correct. The exact words are, "For many years all four remained, till one was stolen away, and that was the image of the young man who pleased the beautiful Alba, who thus relieved him of the spell."
But as there has been always only one devil on the corner, I cannot otherwise reconcile the story with the fact.

I have said that this tale is ancient from intrinsic evidence. Such extravagant alliances of friendship as is here described were actually common in the Middle Ages; they existed in England even till the time of Queen Elizabeth. In "Shakespeare and his Friends," or in the "Youth of Shakespeare"- I forget which- two young men are represented as fighting a duel because each declared that he loved the other most. There was no insane folly of sentiment which was not developed in those days. But this is so foreign to modern ideas, that I think it could only have existed in tradition to these our times.

There were also during the Middle Ages strange heretical sects, among whom such communism existed, like the polyandria of the ancient Hindoos. There may be a trace of it in this story.

Alba, Albina, or Bellaria, appear in several Tuscan traditions. They are forms of the Etruscan Alpan, the fairy of the Dawn, a sub-form of Venus, the spirit of Light and Flowers, described in my work on "Etruscan Roman Traditions." It may be remarked as an ingenious touch in the tale, that she always appears at the first dawn, or at three o'clock, and vanishes with broad day. This distinguishes her from the witches and evil spirits, who always come at midnight and vanish at three o'clock.

The readiness with which the young men consented to assume the forms of demons is easily explained. They understood that it meant only a disguise, and it was very common in the Middle Ages for lovers to wear something strange in honour of their mistresses. The dress of a devil would only seem a joke to the habitués of the Cavolaia. It may be also borne in mind that in other tales of Florence it is distinctly stated that spirits confined in statues, columns, et cetera, only inhabit them "as bees live in hives." They appear to sleep in them by day, and come out at night. So in India the

The Devil Of The Mercato Vecchio

saint or demon only comes into the relic or image from time to time, or when invoked.

After I had written the foregoing, I was so fortunate as to receive from Maddalena yet another legend of the bronze imp of Giovanni di Bologna, which tale she had unearthed in the purlieus of the Mercato Vecchio. I have often met her when thus employed, always in the old part of the town, amid towering old buildings bearing shields of the Middle Ages, or in dusky vicoli and chiassi, and when asked what she was doing, 'twas ever the same reply, "Ma, Signore Carlo, there's an old woman- or somebody- lives here who knows a story." And then I knew that there was going to be a long colloquy in dialect which would appal any one who only knew choice Italian, the end of which would be the recovery, perhaps from half-a-dozen vecchie, of a legend like the following, of which I would premise that it was not translated by me, but by Miss Roma Lister, who knew Maddalena, having taken lessons from her in the sublime art of battezare le carte, or telling fortunes by cards, and other branches of the black art. And having received the manuscript, which was unusually illegible and troublesome, I asked Miss Lister to kindly transcribe it, but with great kindness she translated the whole, only begging me to mention that it is given with the most scrupulous accuracy, word for word, from the original, so far as the difference of language permitted.

The Devil Of The Mercato Vecchio

IL DIAVOLINO DEL CANTO DE' DIAVOLI

The Imp of the Devil's Corner and the Pious Fairy

"There was once a pious fairy who employed all her time in going about the streets of Florence in the shape of a woman, preaching moral sermons for the good of her hearers, and singing so sweetly that all who heard her voice fell in love with her. Even the women forgot to be jealous, so charming was her voice, and dames and damsels followed her about, trying to learn her manner of singing.

"Now the fairy had converted so many folk from their evil ways, that a certain devil or imp- who also had much business in Florence about that time- became jealous of the intruder, and swore to avenge himself; but it appears that there was as much love as hate in the fiend's mind, for the fairy's beautiful voice had worked its charm even when the hearer was a devil. Now, besides being an imp of superior intelligence, he was also an accomplished ventriloquist (or one who could imitate strange voices as if sounding afar or in any place); so one day while the pious fairy in the form of a beautiful maiden held forth to an admiring audience, two voices were heard in the street, one here, another there, and the first sang:

> "Senti o bella una parola,
> Te la dico a te sola,
> Qui nessun ci puo'l sentire
> Una cosa ti vuo dire;
> Se la senti la stemperona,
> L'a un voce da buffona
> Tiene in mano la corona.

The Devil Of The Mercato Vecchio

Per fare credere a questo o quella,
Che l'e sempre una verginella.'

"'Hear, O lovely maid, a word,
Only to thyself I'd bear it,
For it must not be o'erheard,
Least of all should the preacher hear it.
'Tis that, while seeming pious, she,
Holding in hand a rosary,
Her talk is all hypocrisy,
To make believe to simple ears,
That still the maiden wreath she wears.'

"Then another voice answered:

"'La risposta ti vuo dare,
Senza farti aspettare;
Ora di un bell' affare,
Te la voglio raccontare,
Quella donna che sta a cantare,
E una Strega di queste contrade,

Che va da questo e quello,
A cantarle indovinello,
A chi racconta: Voi siete
Buona donna affezionata.
Al vostro marito, ma non sapete,
Cie' di voi un 'altra appasionata.'

"'Friends, you'll not have long to wait
For what I'm going to relate;
And it is a pretty story
Which I am going to lay before ye.
That dame who singing there you see
Is a witch of this our Tuscany,
Who up and down the city flies,
Deceiving people with her lies,
Saying to one: The truth to tell,
I know you love your husband well;
But you will find, on close inspection,
Another has his fond affection.'

The Devil Of The Mercato Vecchio

"In short, the imp, by changing his voice artfully, and singing his ribald songs everywhere, managed in the end to persuade people that the fairy was no better than she should be, and a common mischief-maker and disturber of domestic peace. So the husbands, becoming jealous, began to quarrel with their wives, and then to swear at the witch who led them astray or put false suspicion into their minds.

"But it happened that the fairy was in high favour with a great saint, and going to him, she told all her troubles and the wicked things which were said of her, and besought him to free her good name from the slanders which the imp of darkness had spread abroad (l'aveva chalugnato).

"Then the saint, very angry, changed the devil into a bronze figure (mascherone, an architectural ornament), but first compelled him to go about to all who had been influenced by his slanders, and undo the mischief which he had made, and finally to make a full confession in public of everything, including his designs on the beautiful fairy, and how he hoped by compromising her to lead her to share his fate.

"Truly the imp cut but a sorry figure when compelled to thus stand up in the Old Market place at the corner of the Palazzo Cavolaia before a vast multitude and avow all his dirty little tricks; but he contrived withal to so artfully represent his passionate love for the fairy, and to turn all his sins to that account, that many had compassion on him, so that indeed among the people, in time, no one ever spoke ill of the doppio povero diavolo, or doubly poor devil, for they said he was to be pitied since he had no love on earth and was shut out of heaven.

"Nor did he quite lose his power, for it was said that after he had been confined in the bronze image, if any one spoke ill of him or said, 'This is a devil, and as a devil he can never enter Paradise,' then the imp would persecute that man with strange voices and sounds until such time as the offender should betake himself to the Palazzo della Cavolaia, and there, standing before the bronze image, should ask his pardon.

"And if it pleased the Diavolino, he forgave them, and they had peace; but if it did not, they were pursued by the double mocking voice which made dialogue or sang duets over all their sins and follies and disgraces. And whether they stayed at home or went abroad, the voices were ever about them, crying aloud or tittering and whispering or hissing, so that they had no rest by day or night; and this is what befell all who spoke ill of the Diavolino del Canto dei Diavoli."

The Devil Of The Mercato Vecchio

* * * * *

The saint mentioned in this story was certainly Pietro Martire or Peter the Martyrer, better deserving the name of murderer, who, preaching at the very corner where the bronze imp was afterwards placed, declared that he beheld the devil, and promptly exorcised him. There can be little doubt that the image was placed there to commemorate this probably "pious fraud."

It is only since I wrote all this that I learned that there were formerly two of these devils, one having been stolen not many years ago. This verifies to some extent the consistency of the author of the legend, "The Devil of the Mercato Vecchio," who says there were four.

There is a very amusing and curious trait of character manifested in the conclusion of this story which might escape the reader's attention were it not indicated. It is the vindication of the "puir deil," and the very evident desire to prove that he was led astray by love, and that even the higher spirit could not take away all his power. Here I recognise beyond all question the witch, the fortune-teller and sorceress, who prefers Cain to Abel, and sings invocations to the former, and to Diana as the dark queen of the Strege, and always takes sides with the heretic and sinner and magian and goblin. It is the last working of the true spirit of ancient heathenism, for the fortune-tellers, and especially those of the mountains, all come of families who have been regarded as enemies by the Church during all the Middle Ages, and who are probably real and direct descendants of Canidia and her contemporaries, for where this thing is in a family it never dies out. I have a great many traditions in which the hand of the heathen witch and the worship of "him who has been wronged" and banished to darkness, is as evident as it is here.

Legends Of Florence

* * * * *

"Which indeed seems to show," comments the learned Flaxius, "that if the devil is never quite so black as he is painted, yet, on the other hand, he is so far from being of a pure white- as the jolly George Sand boys, such as Heine and Co., thought- that it is hard to make him out of any lighter hue than mud and verdigris mixed. In medio tutissimus ibis. 'Tis also to be especially noted, that in this legend- as in Shelley's poem- the Devil appears as a meddling wretch who is interested in small things, and above all, as given to gossip.

The Devil Of The Mercato Vecchio

"The Devil sat down in London town
Before earth's morning ray,
With a favourite imp he began to chat,
On religion, and scandal, and this and that,
Until the dawn of day."

Legends Of Florence

The Devil Of The Mercato Vecchio

Printed in Great Britain
by Amazon